Not-So-Grizzly Bear Stories

For Mark and Vicky
T.W.

First published in the United States 1998 by
Little Tiger Press
N16 W23390 Stoneridge Drive, Waukesha, WI 53188
Originally published in Great Britain 1997 by
Orchard Books, London
Text copyright © Hiawyn Oram 1997
Illustrations copyright © Tim Warnes 1997
All rights reserved.
Library of Congress Cataloging-in-Publication Data
Oram, Hiawyn.
Not-so-grizzly bear stories / Hiawyn Oram ;
illustrated by Tim Warnes.   p.   cm.
Summary : Ten tales about bears, from the folklore of Lapland, China,
Hungary, Canada, Russia, Japan, North America, Germany, and France.
ISBN 1-888444-41-X
1. Tales. 2. Bears–Folklore.   [1. Folklore. 2. Bears–Folklore.]
I. Warnes, Tim, ill. II. Title.
PZ8.063No   1998   398.24'52978–dc21
98-17388 CIP AC
Printed in Singapore
First American Edition
1 3 5 7 9 10 8 6 4 2

Not-So-Grizzly Bear Stories

Hiawyn Oram

Illustrated by Tim Warnes

LITTLE TIGER PRESS

CONTENTS

Not-So-Hungry Bear

Fox had stolen a fat trout from a Lapp's larder, and now he was enjoying it.

He crunched every bone . . . slowly.

He chewed every mouthful . . . slowly.

After every mouthful he licked his lips . . . slowly.

Bear came by and sniffed.

"That trout smells delicious, friend Fox!"

"That's because it *is* delicious, friend Bear!"

Bear came closer.

Winter had arrived suddenly, and it had been a long time since he'd tasted fish.

"I don't suppose you'd give me a teeny tiny mouthful?" he suggested shyly.

"You're right," said Fox. "I won't. If you want fish, go catch it yourself."

"But everything's frozen. There's no fishing to be done anywhere," said Bear. "And I'm *so* hungry!"

Fox looked at Bear over the last of the trout. He licked his paws . . . slowly.

He narrowed his eyes.

What a stupid creature, he thought to himself, lumbering around, getting on my nerves. I'll teach him to be so helpless.

He moved closer and studied Bear's long, bushy tail—in those days bears had long, bushy tails.

"Taking care of one's hunger during winter is all a matter of practice," Fox said slyly. "If you'd care to meet me here at midnight, out of the kindness of my heart I will show you how to fish."

Bear felt a warm, grateful glow.

Fox was not known for his kindness or generosity, but being naturally trusting, Bear was not in the least suspicious.

"That is the nicest thing anyone has offered to do for me in a long time," he mumbled. "I'll see you here at midnight."

At midnight the cold was even colder. The ice was even thicker.

Bear's teeth were chattering, but he dragged himself from his cave and went to meet Fox.

Fox was waiting impatiently.

"Now," said Fox, "to eat fish all winter, you must start by digging a hole in the ice. Come on, get to it."

Bear got to it as best he could.

Though his paws were freezing and his tummy was empty, he dug away at the thick, hard ice. Finally, he broke through to the water below.

"Good," said Fox. "Now, the trick here is starlight. Fish are attracted to it. Soon they'll come along, pushing and shoving, trying to see the stars. All you have to do is drop your long, bushy tail into the water. Go on, get to it."

Shivering hard, Bear followed Fox's instructions.

"Oh my, oh mercy!" he cried as the freezing water gripped his tail.

Fox stifled a laugh.

"The worst is almost over. Any moment now you'll feel the fish grabbing hold of your tail. As soon as you think you've caught enough, just draw it out and there you are—no longer a hungry winter bear."

Bear was sure he could already feel something tugging at his tail. "It is really very kind of you to show me this fishing trick. Ouch! Er, I can't understand . . . ooh . . . that was a big tug! Do you know, I can't understand why you have such a . . . ouch . . . bad reputation for being mean and sly."

"Nor I," chortled Fox.

"And do you know," Bear went on, "my tail is getting so heavy, I think I may have already caught enough fish for an enormous meal."

"For a bear like you," said Fox, "there's no such thing as an enormous meal. Just hold on there a little longer."

So Bear sat with his tail in the freezing water. And it *was*  freezing. It was gradually freezing solid!

But each time Bear said he was so hungry he'd have to pull his tail out and eat, Fox persuaded him to hold on a little longer. Finally, when Fox was sure that the ice would be solid, he pretended he had to go.

"Oh my goodness! Is that the time? I promised my wife I'd be home by now. I'd better be off or I'll be in for a scolding. Good eating to you, friend Bear—and may your fishing always be so lucky!"

And with that Fox scampered off, laughing to himself, across the ice to the nearest village.

There he woke the dogs by chasing the chickens. Then he ran back across the ice, leading the dogs straight for Bear.

When Bear saw the yapping dogs, he was terrified.
He forgot fishing. He forgot fish. He forgot hunger.

His only thought was to RUN!

But what was this?

He couldn't run. He couldn't move.

His long, bushy tail was frozen solid in the lake,
just as Fox had intended!

He began to tug and pull and yank.

How he tugged and pulled and yanked!

And at last, in the nick of time, he tugged and pulled and yanked so hard he broke free.

But his tail didn't.

His tail stayed right where it was, and when spring came and the ice thawed, it turned into a marmot and ran away.

And there are still those who think that's why bears have such funny little stumps for tails. And why, when winter comes, bears are heard to say . . .

"I think I'll sleep this one out, since, you know, I don't really feel that hungry after all."

A Story from Lapland

Not-So-White Bears

It was a long time ago—so long ago that everything was still young. The earth was young, the stars were young, the forests were young.

The leopards in the forests were so young they had no spots. The deer were so young they had no antlers. The snakes were so young they had no fangs. The tortoises were so young they had no shells, and the bears were so young their fur was still as white as newly fallen snow.

And since all the animals were so young, they all played together.

They didn't hide from one another or run from one another or prey on one another.

And Leopard Cub, Little Deer, and Bear Cub were the best of friends.

They played together from dawn to dusk.

They ate together.

If one got lost, the others soon found him.

If one got a thorn in his foot, another soon pulled it out with his teeth.

Then one day, Leopard Cub's mother found a few black spots on her plain, golden coat.

A few days later, she found some more.

And a few days later, they appeared on Leopard Cub.

Leopard Cub's mother was very impressed.

She felt older and very proud.

She instructed Leopard Cub to stop playing with Bear Cub and Little Deer.

"They are below us now," she said. "We are beautifully decorated, while they are plain as plain. From now on we keep to ourselves. Our spots make us better than they."

Leopard Cub was very confused. What did he care about spots? All he wanted to do was play with his friends. He tried to run off when his mother wasn't looking, but she seemed to have eyes in the back of her head.

Bear Cub and Little Deer were very disappointed.

"Why doesn't Leopard Cub play with us anymore?" they asked their families.

"Because he's busy," came the untruthful answer. "You know how it is. The Leopards are thinking of moving. But never mind, you two have each other, and we are all still good friends."

But not
for long.

A few days
later, Mr. Deer
noticed some bumps
on his forehead.

They itched a little, so he rubbed
them against a tree, and lo and behold,
they grew bigger.

And the next day bigger and bigger.

And bigger and bigger, until they
were fabulous, fully fledged horns.

Mrs. Deer was very impressed.

She felt older and
very proud.

She instructed Little
Deer to stop playing
with Bear Cub.

"Those Bears are below us now," she said. "Your father is beautifully decorated, even more so than the Leopards if you ask me, while the Bears are so boring and white . . . so utterly plain and white. From now on, child, we keep to ourselves."

And like Leopard Cub, Little Deer was most confused. What did he care about antlers? All he wanted to do was play with his friends.

He tried to run off when his mother wasn't looking, but she seemed to have eyes in the back of her head.

Bear Cub was bitterly disappointed.

"Now Little Deer won't play with me either," he wailed. "Why, why, why?"

"He's probably busy," came the answer. "Mr. and Mrs. Deer are probably thinking of moving, too."

"That's not the reason," said Bear Cub, sitting down on the ground in despair. "It's because the

Leopards have spots and Mr. Deer has horns and we have nothing. We're just white, all white, plain and boring and white!"

Then he began to cry. How he cried!

He even wailed he was crying so hard.

And as he wept and wailed, he beat the ground with his paws, and rubbed his eyes and beat the ground, and rubbed his eyes and beat the ground, and with his grubby, muddy paws he smeared his tears.

When at last he stopped crying, he wasn't a plain white bear at all. He was a white bear with beautiful black legs and black markings on his face.

His family was so impressed that they sat down at once and wept and wailed and beat the ground and rubbed their eyes and beat the ground and smeared their tears, until they, too, were not-so-white.

They were the black-and-white bears we now call pandas.

And the Leopards and the Deer marveled and admired—and at last the young could play together again.

A Story from China

Not-So-Smart Bears

Once there were two bears, Bruno and Brun. They thought they were smart, and they *were* smart, but they couldn't stop arguing about who was the smartest.

"I'm so smart I can find honey where no other bear would think of looking," said Brun.

"And I'm so smart I can catch a fish in a fast-running river with my eyes closed," said Bruno.

"Well, why don't you just agree that you're both smart?" asked Squirrel.

"Because I'm smartest," said Brun.

"No, I'm smartest," said Bruno.

And so the argument went on—and on and on.
Sometimes all you could hear in the forest was Brun and Bruno bickering.

"I'm smartest . . ."

"*I'm* smartest . . ."

"But everyone knows *I'm* smartest . . ."

"No, everyone knows *I'm* smartest . . ."

At last one day the other animals could bear it no longer.

"Oh, for goodness sake," said Great Deer. "Why don't you two just go out into the world and find out who is smartest and settle the matter once and for all?"

"Done," said Brun.

"First thing tomorrow," said Bruno.

So early next morning, off the two bears went— out into the world.

The first place they came to was a fast-running river.

"I'm so smart I cross a fast-running river like this," said Brun.

"Well, *I'm* so smart I cross a fast-running river like this," said Bruno.

So Brun crossed the river his way.

And Bruno crossed the river *his* way.

Neither got too wet.

Both made it safely across.

And still they argued.

"Of course, mine was the better way," said Brun. "Much quicker."

"No, no, mine was the better way. Just as quick and certainly safer. But that's to be expected, since of the two of us, I'm the smartest."

And off they went again—on and on and on— arguing and bickering all the way through the fields until they came to a road.

But then they stopped, for there on the side of the road lay something that neither of them had ever seen before.

A big round yellow cheese.

"What's that?" said Brun.

"Don't you know?" said Bruno.

"Do you?" said Brun.

"Of course I know," said Bruno, not wanting to admit he didn't know. "It smells good enough to eat, and I'm very hungry."

"I'm hungrier," said Brun.

"Well, *I'm* so hungry I can't even argue about it," said Bruno. "The question is, how shall we divide it so that you don't get more than I?"

"Or you more than I," said Brun.

"Well, since I'm the smartest, I'll divide it," said Bruno.

"No, no, *I'm* the smartest, so I'll divide it," said Brun.

And off they went again—on and on and on—squabbling and bickering and getting hungrier and hungrier.

Finally, from out of the bushes at the side of the road stepped Red Fox—Sly Red Fox.

"Good morning to you, good bears. What a quandary you seem to be in on the matter of how to share this cheese. Perhaps I can be of assistance. Here, why don't I divide it, and then you'll both see that each piece is exactly the same."

Since they were now starving, the bears agreed, and Sly Red Fox broke the cheese in two.

But she was not called sly for nothing.

She broke it in such a way that one piece was much bigger than the other.

And of course the bears noticed.

"That piece is bigger!"

So Sly Red Fox took a bite out of the bigger piece.

"Now that piece is smaller!"

So Sly Red Fox took a bite out of the other piece.

"Now that piece is bigger!"

So Sly Red Fox took another bite out of the first piece.

"Now that piece is smaller!"

And on and on and on she went, until there was nothing left of either piece but two small crumbs.

"Oh well," Fox sighed, slyly wiping her mouth with the back of a red paw. "Enjoy your equal crumbs . . ."

And off she slunk back into the bushes at the side of the road to lick her lips and sleep.

Brun and Bruno looked at each other.

"Not very smart," said Brun.

"Not very smart at all," said Bruno.

"I feel like a real fool," said Brun.

"So do I," said Bruno. "What shall we tell the others when we get back to the forest?"

"We'll tell them," said Brun, "that we went into the world and discovered there is no difference between us—one of us can be as smart as the other."

"And as foolish as the other," said Bruno.

"Good thinking," they said together, and they shook paws and returned to the forest, which never again rang with the sound of . . .

"I'm smartest."

"No, *I'm* smartest."

"No, *I'm* smartest!"

A Story from Hungary

Not-So-Strange Bears

 nce long ago there was an Eskimo couple named Tuk and Topkin. Not long after Tuk and Topkin got married, Topkin gave birth to twin boys.

Tuk was very excited about his newborn sons.

Topkin was proud, but she tilted her head to one side and said, "They're a bit hairy, don't you think? Unusually hairy?"

"Oh, they'll grow out of that," cried Tuk, and he took two bracelets of plaited sealskin and placed one around each of his sons' wrists. "With these bracelets, my children, I name you both Nanook!"

And so the two little Nanooks became part of Tuk and Topkin's family.

But though they grew sturdy, they didn't grow less hairy.

If anything they grew *more* hairy.

"I don't know," sighed Topkin. "It's not that I don't love them. But sometimes they don't really seem like they're mine."

"They're yours all right and mine all right and ours all right!" said Tuk. "Look how strong they are and how well they crawl and tumble and play together!"

But one morning disaster struck . . .

When Topkin went to wake the twins, they weren't under their blankets.

They weren't in the igloo.

"They must have crawled outside!" she cried.

But outside it was snowing hard, and there was no sign of the two Nanooks.

"They're so little," Tuk called over the storm. "They can't have gone far. I'll take the sled and look for them. Don't worry, they'll be home soon."

So Tuk got out his sled and dogs and set off in search of his sons.

But when he returned, he returned alone and held Topkin tight. "For two days and nights, I've searched. It is beyond me where they might have gone."

"Maybe for now," said Topkin through her tears. "But I know we shall see them again."

And time went by and life went on, and Topkin gave birth to another son and then another son— Maleyato and Apukeena. They didn't crawl away in the night but grew up to be fine young men.

And one day the grown Maleyato went seal hunting on the icebergs, and the grown Apukeena went caribou hunting on the plains.

But both got into trouble.

The iceberg under Maleyato's feet cracked, and the piece he was standing on began to float toward the open sea.

Meanwhile, out on the bare plains the wolves got wind of Apukeena's dogs and chased them off, leaving Apukeena lost in land he didn't know.

Back on the iceberg, a great white tower of a creature suddenly appeared beside Maleyato.

"However terrifying I look, don't be afraid," said the tower. "My name is Nanook and I am your brother. Hold on, and I'll take you home."

Far away on the plains, a great brown tower of a creature appeared beside Apukeena and said almost the same thing.

"I may seem terrifying, but don't be afraid. My name is Nanook and I am your brother. Hold on to me, and I'll show you the way home."

And when the two great creatures brought Maleyato and Apukeena close to the family igloo, they each handed over a plaited sealskin bracelet.

"Take these to our mother and tell her we ask her forgiveness for disappearing all those years ago. And tell her to be proud, for whether she knows it or not, her firstborn became the first bears."

"Nanook the White, that's me," said the white tower.

"And Nanook the Brown, that's me," said the other tower.

And when Maleyato and Apukeena, still shocked and shaken by their encounters, went into the igloo and showed Topkin the bracelets, she jumped up and down with joy.

"I knew it! I knew it! I knew we'd see them again."

Then she called Tuk, and together they ran out into the snow, just in time to watch proudly as Nanook the White and Nanook the Brown ambled off—each in his own direction.

To Tuk and Topkin, they didn't seem strange or towering or terrifying at all—just two big, very beautiful bears.

A Story from Canada

Not-So-Selfish Bear

Once there was a very lonely Bear.
How lonely I am in this dark and quiet forest, he thought to himself. If only there was someone here just for me.

One day while he was picking and eating berries, he saw just that someone.

She was small and bright-eyed and picking and eating berries, too.

As she picked she sang.

Sometimes she stopped to chase butterflies or talk to the warblers.

Sometimes she even
stopped to talk to herself.
Enchanting! thought Bear
as he watched her. And what
good company she would make!
And without giving a thought to
the girl's wishes, Bear sprang into the
clearing, picked her up, and carried her off.

The girl kicked and screamed.

"Put me down, you bad Bear! Put me down. Take
me back. You have no right to carry me off!"

"Don't worry," said Bear when they reached his den. "The last thing I would ever do is harm you. It's just that I've been so lonely in this deep, dark forest. But with you here to sing to me and talk with me and join me at mealtimes, I won't be lonely anymore. Now, tell me, what is your name?"

"Goldenhair!" The little girl stamped her foot. "My name is Goldenhair. And what if I don't want to keep you company? And what about my parents? They'll think I've been eaten by someone like you and then there'll be no stopping their tears."

"I can't help that," said Bear. "Now, sing me a song while I prepare supper, and don't ever try to run away, or someone like me will most certainly eat you."

Goldenhair—who though she was young was also very sensible—decided she would do as she was told, for the time being anyway.

So every day she sang and talked and showed Bear the things she knew.

She showed him how to make daisy chains.

She showed him how to whistle and play cat's cradle with a piece of string she had in her pocket.

Bear was delighted with her company.

He made her a bed of soft moss, and he brought her the best honeycombs.

"I am the happiest bear in the world," he said, "except when I hear you crying at night. Why do you cry so much when we have such an interesting life together?"

Goldenhair explained that she cried for her parents.

"Their hearts will be broken. By now they will be certain I've been gobbled up by a bear or a wolf."

"Very well," said Bear. "If it will stop your crying, I'll visit them and see that they are all right."

Goldenhair saw her chance.

"Would you? Would you do that? And would you take them something from me so they will know I'm alive and well?"

"If you like," said Bear.

So Goldenhair sent Bear off to get flour from the village baker and a basket and some fresh white linen from the village weaver.

Then she set about baking a batch of blackberry pies.

And while she baked, she lectured Bear.

"Now, you listen to me, Bear," she said. "You take the basket to my parents, but on no account are you to touch or eat a single pie on the way. Do you understand? Because if you do, I shall see you, and you'll be sorry."

"Sure," said Bear. "I understand."

When the pies were ready and Bear wasn't looking, Goldenhair climbed into the basket and covered herself with pies and the piece of fresh white linen.

Then Bear picked up the basket and set off.

He found the basket surprisingly heavy, so after a few miles he set it down.

"Hmm," he said, stretching. "I've walked far enough. Perhaps I'll take a seat and just a single pie I'll eat."

Immediately Goldenhair called out from inside the basket, "I see you, Bear. I see you there. And don't you dare!"

Bear nearly jumped out of his skin.

"What very good eyes she must have if she can still see me!"

And he hurriedly picked up the basket and set off.

But when he had walked another few miles, he found the basket so heavy he had to set it down again.

"Phew!" he wiped his brow. "I've come so far, perhaps I'll take a seat and one single pie I'll eat."

Immediately Goldenhair called out, "I see you, Bear. I see you there. And don't you dare!"

Bear nearly jumped out of his skin again.

"What very, *very* good eyes she must have if she can still see me!"

And quaking a little, he picked up the basket and did not stop walking until he reached Goldenhair's house.

There he put the basket down on the porch and banged on the door, calling out, "A message from your daughter, Goldenhair!"

Then, since he could hear the household dogs barking and tugging on their chains, he ran as fast as he could back to the forest.

And as soon as Bear was gone, Goldenhair jumped out of her hiding place in the basket and threw herself into her parents' arms.

And though some say that was the end of the story, actually it wasn't.

A few weeks later, as Goldenhair sat by the kitchen stove, she heard a tapping at the window.

When she looked out, there was Bear.

"It's all right," he said. "I've just come to say good-bye and thank you for your good company. Just the memory of it means I'll never be so lonely again."

Then he blew her a kiss, tossed a small leather pouch into the kitchen, and lumbered on his way.

To Goldenhair and her parents' amazement, the leather pouch was full of gold.

They were now rich—and all thanks to a very generous bear.

A Story from Russia

Not-So-Grisly Bear

Once there was a Crescent Moon Bear who lived at the top of a tall mountain.

When he got angry, rabbits ran, foxes fled, eagles scattered, and even the clouds quivered.

"And that's fine by me," he said to himself. "Because that's what I am, a great, grisly Crescent Moon Bear. A rager, a roarer, a growler. So let everyone know it and no one come near."

And no one did come near.

He stood at the entrance to his cave and roared, "I am *the* great and *the* grisly Crescent Moon Bear. When I roar, rabbits run, foxes flee, eagles scatter, and even the clouds quiver. So let everyone leave me be."

And everyone did leave him be—with his growls and his rage and his roars and his grisliness for company.

Then one day, as he was thinking of going out for an evening meal, he heard a rustling in the bushes outside his cave.

His eyes glittered with rage. A growl grew in his throat. A pounce pulsed in his paws, but he choked back a

roar . . . for even before he had gone outside, he smelled a freshly cooked something . . .

Suspiciously, he put his nose outside the cave.

On the path lay a rice paper parcel.

He sniffed the parcel . . . the air . . . the parcel . . .
. . . the air. He went inside and growled,
"Who dares come so close?"

He put his nose outside the cave
and sniffed again . . . the freshly
cooked food in the parcel . . .
the delicious steam coming
from it . . . the air . . .
the food . . . the steam . . . the air
. . . the food . . . *and he gobbled it*
all up in one gulp.

Then he stood on his
hind legs and gave such a
roar that rabbits ran, foxes
fled, eagles scattered, and
the clouds quivered—this
was a warning to whoever
had dared come so close,
never to do so again.

But the next day, as he was thinking of going out for his evening meal, he heard the same rustling outside his cave.

On the path was another parcel. Suspiciously, he sniffed the parcel . . . the delicious steam . . . the air . . . the parcel . . .

the steam . . . the air.

He went inside and growled, "Who dares bother me at home?"

He put his nose outside and sniffed again . . . the food . . . the steam . . . the air . . . the food . . . the steam . . . the air . . . *and he gobbled it all up in one gulp.*

Then he stood on his hind legs and gave such a roar that rabbits ran, foxes fled, eagles scattered, and the very mountain quivered—this was a warning to whoever had dared come so close, *never* to do so again.

But the next evening, it happened once more.
And the next and the next and the next.

Finally, one evening after Crescent Moon Bear had gobbled up the food in one gulp and stood on his hind legs and roared till the very mountain quivered, he looked down and found himself staring into the terrified face of a woman carrying a bag of supplies.

He dropped down onto all fours and growled his grisliest growl.

"So, it's you who dares do this! Why do you dare? Haven't you heard my warnings? Don't you know who I am? Don't you know I could finish you off in one crunch?"

"Oh, please!" the woman's voice trembled. "My husband is sick, as sick as can be. He refuses to eat. He lives like a wild animal, and the only thing that can cure him is a hair from the crescent moon at your throat. So I have made my way up this mountain and steeled myself against your rage and your grisliness to beg for one . . . just one . . . single hair."

And Crescent Moon Bear reared up and roared, "A hair from the crescent moon at my throat? For your impudence I think I *will* finish you off in one—"

But even as he was leaning forward to crunch her, Crescent Moon Bear found himself looking straight into the woman's eyes—and in that moment he saw such love for her husband and such a longing to cure him that his heart melted.

From head to toe, he was flooded, not with blind rage, but with all-seeing tenderness.

And the moment was long enough for him to gently lift his head, offer his throat, and let the woman pluck out a hair.

Then he gave a deep, low growl and turned and ambled away.

And though it is true he never stopped being great and grisly, something about that moment had changed him. As the rabbits and foxes and eagles noticed, he was never quite so grisly in his growls or quite so rageful in his roars again.

A Story from Japan

Not-So-Greedy Bears

Mr. Bear, Mrs. Bear, and their three children, Big, Medium, and Little, were lucky. They had a lake full of salmon, surrounded by bushes full of cranberries, all to themselves.

"Now," said Mrs. Bear every morning and every evening, "what shall we eat?"

"Salmon!" cried her husband and children. "Fresh, fat, jumping salmon! And after that a few cranberries, and then more salmon!"

Naturally, since the lake was theirs, the Bears did not want anyone else to know about it.

Mr. Bear built a large folding screen and placed it

around the lake. And Mrs. Bear painted the screen to look like just another part of the woods.

"Now," she said when it was done, "who would ever think there was a lake full of fresh, fat, jumping salmon behind that screen?"

"Me!" cried Big, dashing behind the screen and wading into the lake for his supper.

"Me!" yelled Medium, following Big.

"Me!" whooped Little, following Medium.

"Ho, ho, ho," laughed Mr. Bear. "Aren't our children amusing?"

"Most amusing," said Mrs. Bear. "We are fortunate to have them and our own private lake that no one else will ever find."

But as it happened, at that moment Raven was hopping around nearby—in one of his greedy trickster moods.

Hearing the Bear children's whooping, he hopped closer.

Hearing their splashing but seeing no water, he hopped closer and kept on hopping and peering until he found a hole in the screen.

Aha! he thought greedily to himself. The Bears' private lake, teeming with fresh, fat fish and bursting at the edges with bright red cranberries. Oh, give me, give me!

With some difficulty he dragged himself from the wonderful sight, flew into the air, and with a lot of urgent flapping, flew down beside Mr. and Mrs. Bear.

"Raven, dear boy!" said Mr. Bear. "What brings you to our humble abode?"

"Just a bit of news I thought might interest you," said Raven cunningly. "There's a day of games in the far forest tomorrow. All the best games—running races, shot put, discus, high jump, long jump—all the games you and your family love so much and are so good at."

"Games indeed!" said Mrs. Bear, thinking of her children and how they would be bound to win everything. "Well, husband, we will all have to go, will we not?"

"We certainly will," said Mr. Bear, "or our children will never forgive us!"

So early the next morning, the Bears set off for the far forest.

And as soon as they were out of sight, Raven hopped up and eased himself over the screen.

Munch! Crunch! Munch!

Splash! Dip! Dive! Thrash! Munch! And more munch. He feasted as he'd never feasted before.

And the whole time he ate, he kept thinking how wrong it was that the Bears should have such a lake all to themselves.

"Why, everyone should have a share of this— everyone, especially ME!"

Then, in spite of being so stuffed, he had what he thought was a brilliant idea.

"I'll steal the lake!" He put his head to one side thoughtfully. "That's what I'll do. I'll roll it up like a blanket, fold in the edges so the water can't escape, and take it for myself!"

And that evening, when the Bears returned from the forest—exhausted and furious, for they had found no games anywhere—there at the top of a tall pine tree sat Raven, with their precious lake rolled up in his beak!

"Trickster! Greedy trickster!"

Mrs. Bear shook her fist at him.
"Rotten Raven, you'll be sorry!" said the
Bear children, dancing up and down.

Mr. Bear hurled himself at the tree, in the
hopes of bringing it, Raven, and the lake to the
ground. But it didn't work. Raven simply flew
to another tree and another tree and then flew
off all together.

"Oh dear!" wept Mrs. Bear. "Our wonderful
private lake . . . gone. Oh dear! What will we do now?"

"Pack a few things and follow him—to the
ends of the earth if need be—and get it back!"
bellowed Mr. Bear.

"To the ends of the earth!" echoed Big, Medium, and Little.

"To the ends of the earth!" cried Mrs. Bear.

But though the Bears crossed mountains, valleys, and distant plains, they were slow and Raven was fast and always ahead of them or out of reach or nowhere to be seen.

Until at last, much thinner and very hungry, the Bears reached the edge of a green and pleasant valley and looked down—and there it was: their lake, being unrolled by Raven.

Certainly it was smaller, since on its travels a lot of water had leaked away. And certainly there were fewer salmon in it, since some had fallen out with the water. But other than that, no harm had been done— there were still plenty of fish, and the edges still glowed bright red with ripe cranberries.

"Whoopee!" the Bear children cried, running and tumbling toward it.

"Whoopee!" cried Mrs. Bear, quite forgetting herself. "Our lovely lake all to ourselves again."

"I don't think so, my dear," said Mr. Bear. "Not now. Not ours. Not ever again."

And as he spoke, from every direction came beavers and otters and bears and birds, scurrying and scampering and swooping hungrily toward the fat, fresh, jumping salmon and the ripe red cranberries.

"Well," Raven said as he flew over to gloat. "It does serve you right. You never should have tried to keep it to yourselves."

And only a little grumpily, the Bears muttered, "Maybe you have a point . . ."

"There *are* a lot of fish . . ."

"No point in being *that* greedy . . ."

"There really *is* enough in this lake to go around!"

A Story from North America

Not-So-Unlucky Bear

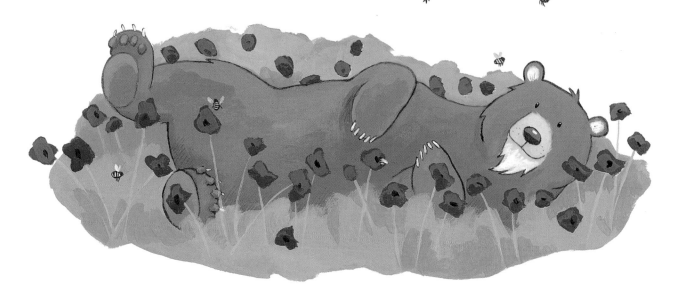

Once there was a bear called Luckybeard, who loved to boast about how lucky he was.

He boasted to his fellow bears. He boasted to the other animals. He boasted to the flowers and the bees.

"Nothing can touch me!" he boasted. "Whatever happens turns in my favor. If I trip, I trip over a pot of gold. In fact, I'm so lucky I'm willing to bet that within the year I'll be married to the king's daughter."

Now, since he was so lucky, no one was prepared to take him up on the bet, but the next day, who should come walking into the forest but the king himself.

"So, what's the buzz?" he asked the bees.

"The buzz, Your Majesty, is that Luckybeard's going to marry your daughter."

"Really?" said the king, concealing his alarm. "And where pray did you hear about that?"

"From Luckybeard himself," buzzed the bees.

"From Luckybeard himself, ha-ha," laughed the king, but inside he was fuming. Over my dead body will that boastful bear get into my family! he thought.

And he went home and came back the next day disguised as an old coffin maker pushing a coffin.

When the king came across Luckybeard, he stopped and called out, "Good day, Bear. Here's two gold pieces if you'll climb into this coffin so I can see if it's right for one as big as you."

"Well, that's lucky," said Luckybeard. "I'm right out of gold. Sure, I'll do that for you, old coffin maker."

But as soon as Luckybeard climbed into the coffin, the king nailed down the lid and pushed it to the bank of the nearest river.

"Marry that!" he cried as he tipped bear and coffin into the water. "And count yourself lucky!"

The king had drilled holes in the coffin so it would quickly fill with water and Luckybeard would drown long before he could marry anyone. But he was not called Luckybeard for nothing.

The river was a fast-flowing river—very fast-flowing—and before the coffin could sink, the current took it downstream, where it got caught in a miller's dam.

"Oh my! Oh my! What have we here?" The miller's wife called her husband. "Cross yourself and find out who's inside it."

So the miller and his boy dragged the coffin from the dam and opened it, and Luckybeard rolled out.

"Well, this is lucky!" he said. "If your mill hadn't been here, I'd have drowned. Now, what can I do for you in return?"

"Hmm," the miller said, looking the bear up and down. "You're a big strong fellow, and I'm getting old and so is my wife, and the boy has barely got a muscle on him. So how about you live here with us and do the heavy work?"

"I will indeed," said Luckybeard, "and count myself lucky."

So Luckybeard moved into the mill and took on all the heavy work.

"You're a gift to us!" said the miller's wife as the mill prospered and she had time to put her feet up. "And part of the family now."

"For which I count myself lucky," said Luckybeard.

But as things happened, not long afterward the king was caught in a heavy storm and had to take shelter in the mill.

He was surprised to see a bear doing the heavy work and inquired where he'd come from.

"A coffin, Your Majesty," said the miller's wife. "It drifted into our dam. Can you imagine that?"

"I think I can," said the king, concealing his alarm. "Now, here are four pieces of gold if you will allow that bear to carry an urgent letter to the palace. But on no account is he to know that the letter is from me or even that I have been here."

"Your wish is our command, Your Majesty," said the miller's wife, and she took the king's letter, which unbeknownst to her went like this . . .

Dearest Queen,

When the bearer of this letter arrives at the palace, have him immediately thrown into the dungeons, never to see the light of day again. (Or our daughter.) Obey in every detail.

Yours ever and with love,

The King

The miller's wife gave it to Luckybeard, saying he should treat the matter with the greatest urgency and hurry back only when he had safely delivered it.

"I will—and count myself lucky to be asked," said Luckybeard as he took off his apron, wiped his face, and set off with the letter for the palace.

But before he reached the palace, he fell and twisted his ankle, and as he lay by the side of the road, who should come along but two robbers.

"Hey-ho, big bad Bear!" they laughed. "What have you got for us? Gold and fancy timepieces?"

"Nothing like that," said Luckybeard. "But it is lucky you've come along, because I have an urgent letter for the palace, and if you let me lean on you for the rest of the way, I'm sure you'll be well rewarded."

But the robbers wanted to see the letter first, and they huddled together to read it.

"This is terrible!" whispered the first. "The king is too cruel!"

"Then let's have some fun and fix him," said the second, getting out his travel pen and ink.

So the robbers wrote another letter, which unbeknownst to Luckybeard went like this . . .

Dearest Queen,
The bearer of this letter
is to marry our daughter
with all pomp and
ceremony immediately.
Obey in every detail, do not
await my return.
All love
The King

They folded it, popped it into Luckybeard's pouch, and helped him along to the palace.

When they arrived and the queen read the letter, the pomp and ceremony began immediately.

Luckybeard was given the best suite.

The robbers were given the second-best.

The royal household went on wedding alert, and the king's daughter was brought to meet the bridegroom.

But when she saw Luckybeard, she wrinkled up her nose and screamed, "Over my dead body will I ever marry that!"

Luckybeard took one look at her, saw she was exactly like her father, forgot about his twisted ankle, and fled—all the way back to the mill.

"I delivered the letter," he panted, "as instructed."

"And what was your reward?" said the miller.

Luckybeard took a deep breath and said, "A very lucky escape!"

A Story from Germany

Not-So-Blue Bear

Once long ago, Bluebird was a gray bird—as gray and dull as a gray rock.

"This is no good for me," she said. "My nature is as clear and bright as the blue sky."

One day she was flying over a lake.

The waters of the lake reflected the sky.

They were as blue as Graybird felt she should be.

She dipped her head in the blue water and examined her reflection.

Still as gray as gray.

Then she noticed a bright blue butterfly fluttering nearby.

"Oh, Butterfly," she said, "tell me how you got to be so blue. I bet it was from dipping into this lake."

"As a matter of fact," replied the butterfly, "it was. And if you follow my instructions exactly for four mornings, then you too can be as blue as the blue lake."

So Graybird listened to Butterfly's instructions and followed them exactly. And on the fourth morning when she fluttered out of the water, there she was—as blue as the bright, cloudless sky. She was about to fly away and show the world when she remembered Butterfly's last instruction.

"Blue lake, blue lake," she sang,
"Thanks with all my heart,
Oh, thanks in every way,
For giving me such beauty,
And turning me from gray."

Then and only then did she fly off to admire herself in every pool and stream she came to.

A few days later, as she preened on the edge of the

lake, along came Black Bear.

"Oh my, oh my, Bluebird!" he marveled. "As I remember it, you were very recently a gray bird!"

"True," warbled Bluebird, "but not anymore!"

Black Bear sat down and took a good look at Bluebird. He looked down at his own fur.

And deep in his big shy heart, a thought occurred to him.

If I were as blue as Bluebird, perhaps I'd stop being so shy. Perhaps I'd be able to preen and sing and show off. Perhaps if my appearance changed, I'd change with it!

And now that the thought had occurred to him, Black Bear couldn't get rid of it. It buzzed around him like a fly. Finally, very shyly, he spoke up.

"Um, Bluebird," he mumbled, "I don't suppose you'd share the secret of how you turned from dull gray to beautiful blue, would you?"

"Well, why not? Butterfly shared it with me," trilled Bluebird. "If you listen carefully and follow my instructions exactly, then you too can be as blue as blue."

So Black Bear listened carefully and followed Butterfly's instructions.

He bathed in the blue water of the lake four times for four mornings.

First facing north.
Then facing south.
Then facing east.
Then facing west.

Each time he sang a song asking the lake for a little of its blue.

"Blue lake, blue lake," he sang,
"Just enough to paint this fur
That makes me dark and shy.
Share with me your lovely blue,
And Blue Bear will be I!"

And on the fourth morning when he ambled out of the water, there he was—not Black Bear at all but Blue Bear—as bright and blue as the cloudless sky.

"Oh my, oh my!" he cried. "This really is something, isn't it?"

He stared at his reflection in the lake.

He blushed at his new blue beauty.

Then he rushed off to find Buffalo and Wolf and Coyote and see if, for once in his life, he could manage a little preening and showing off.

"Oh, black Buffalo, gray Wolf, and gray Coyote!" he cried when he found them. "Isn't it amazing? Have you ever seen anything like it?"

He stood on his hind legs and did his best to prance.

"Even the ears! Even the claws! What do you think, my friends? What do you think?" Buffalo and Wolf and Coyote stared at him as if he'd gone mad.

"Isn't *what* amazing?" asked Buffalo.

"Even the ears, what?" asked Wolf.

"Even the claws, what?" asked Coyote.

Then Bear looked down at himself in dismay. There was the faintest tinge of blue at the tips of his claws. But the rest of him was as black as black bark on a moonless night.

And at that moment Bluebird flew up and perched on one of Buffalo's horns.

"Oh, Bear!" she trilled breathlessly. "I said to follow my instructions exactly!"

"But I did," said Bear, sitting down in a heap of disappointment. "Didn't I? Four times each morning, facing north, facing south . . ."

But even as the words came out of his mouth, he remembered. He'd done everything to get what he wanted from the lake but had forgotten to sing his thanks on the fourth morning.

Then very slowly he got up and ambled off into the dark woods to think. And soon he had decided he was Black Bear after all, not Blue Bear. That's the way it was. That's the way it always would be.

"And considering I am shy and not a show-off," he sighed, "that's the way it always *should* be."

A Story from North America

Not-So-Lowly Bear

Once there was a king who couldn't stop spending.

He spent everything he had.

Then he started borrowing.

One day, riding through the forest, he saw Bruin the Bear sitting on a sack of gold.

"Lowly bear, lowly bear," he said, "in case you don't know it, I am the king, and I need some money. Lend me that sack of gold."

Bruin got up and bowed.

"Well, why not, Your Majesty. I haven't much use for gold at the moment. If you can repay it within the year, I'll gladly lend it to you."

"On that you have my word," said the king.

Well, a year went by and then another, and the king, who had long since spent the gold, made no effort to repay the generous Bruin.

And Bruin grew uneasy.

"Just because he's a king, that's no reason not to keep his word," he said, and off he set to see the king and try to get his money back.

Now, he hadn't gone far when who should he meet but Frederick the Fox.

"Hello, friend Frederick," said Bruin.

"Hello, friend Bruin," said the fox. "And where are you going this fine morning?"

"To see the king and get my money back," said Bruin.

"Then let me come with you," said the fox.

"Very well," said Bruin. "But it's a long way, and you will get tired. So make yourself small, jump into my big spacious belly, and I will carry you."

So Frederick the Fox jumped into Bruin the Bear's big spacious belly, and off they set to see the king and try to get Bruin's money back.

They hadn't gone far when who should they meet but Longlegs the Ladder.

"Hello, friend Longlegs," said Bruin.

"Hello, friend Bruin," said the ladder. "And where are you going this fine morning?"

"To see the king and get my money back," said Bruin.

"Then let me come with you," said the ladder.

"Very well," said Bruin. "But it's a long way, and your legs are stiff. So make yourself small, jump into my enormously spacious belly, and I will carry you."

So Longlegs the Ladder joined Frederick the Fox inside Bruin the Bear, and off they set to see the king and try to get Bruin's money back.

They hadn't gone far when who should they meet but Runalong the River.

"Hello, friend Runalong," said Bruin.

"Hello, friend Bruin," said the river. "And where are you going this fine morning?"

"To see the king and get my money back," said Bruin.

"Then let me come with you," said the river.

"Very well," said Bruin. "But it's a long way, and you will dry yourself out. So make yourself small, jump into my humungously spacious belly, and I will carry you."

So Runalong the River joined Longlegs the Ladder and Frederick the Fox inside Bruin the Bear, and off they set to see the king and try to get Bruin's money back.

They hadn't gone far when who should they meet but Whineround the Wasps' Nest.

"Hello, friend Whineround," said Bruin.

"Hello, friend Bruin," said the wasps' nest. "And where are you going this fine morning?"

"To see the king and get my money back," said Bruin.

"Then let me come with you," said the wasps' nest.

"Very well," said Bruin. "But it's a long way, and you have no legs at all. So make yourself small, jump into my big and humungously spacious belly, and I will carry you."

So, Whineround the Wasps' Nest joined Runalong the River, Longlegs the Ladder, and Frederick the Fox inside Bruin the Bear, and off they set to see the king and try to get Bruin's money back.

Some time later Bruin and his full belly arrived at the king's castle, and Bruin rang the bell. But when

the doorkeeper announced him, the king refused to
see him.

"I bet he wants his money back," he roared.
"Have him put in with the geese.
With a bit of luck, they'll peck
him to pieces, and that'll be the
end of the whole business."

So the king's courtiers put
Bruin in with
the geese. But
Bruin remembered
who was inside
him and cried,

"Hurry out, Fred Fox, my friend,
Or pecked to bits will be my end!"

And Frederick leapt from Bruin's spacious belly
and chased the geese right out of the kingdom.

"Then throw him down the well!" ordered the king when he heard what happened. "With a bit of luck, he'll drown, and that'll be the end of this whole business."

So the king's courtiers threw Bruin down the well. But Bruin remembered who else was inside him and cried,

"Hurry, Longlegs, faithful friend,
Or drubbed and drowned will be my end!"

And Longlegs leapt out of Bruin's spacious belly, laid herself against the side of the well, and let Bruin climb to safety.

"Then throw him into the furnace!" ordered the king when he heard what happened. "With a bit of luck, he'll burn, and that'll be the end of the whole business."

So the king's courtiers threw Bruin into the furnace. But Bruin remembered who else was inside him and cried,

"Hurry out, Runalong, my friend,
Or burned to cinders is my end!"

And Runalong jumped out of Bruin's spacious belly and rushed into the furnace to put out the fire.

"Very well! Bring him to me!" ordered the king when he heard what happened. "And I will end the whole business myself!"

So the king's courtiers dragged Bruin into the throne room.

And the king drew his sword.

And all his courtiers drew their swords.

"On guard!" said the king.

But Bruin stayed calm and cried,

"Hurry, Whineround, hurry friend,

Or this will surely be my end!"

And Whineround the Wasps' Nest jumped out of Bruin's spacious belly, letting loose

an army of wasps who stung the king and his courtiers so hard that that was the end of them.

And when word got around, the king's subjects flocked to the palace to congratulate Bruin.

"To Bruin the Bear and friends!" they roared. "Ten times more worthy than the spendthrift king he has rid us of!"

Then they lifted the fallen king's crown from the floor and placed it on Bruin's head.

And no one was surprised to find it fitted perfectly.

A Story from France

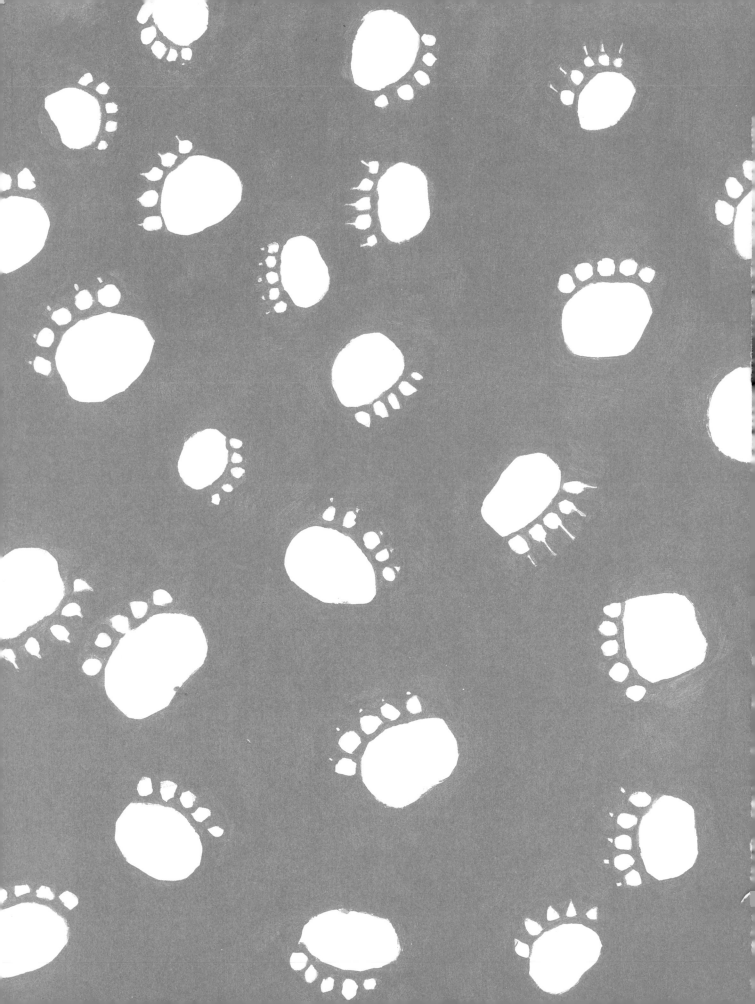